Here is a story all about li
How I carry on as that i
I try my hardest in everyth
But sometimes I fail and that makes me blue
It's a lonely world out here all on my own
To me it's real. All that I have known
I have a loving family and that I am blessed
They may drive me mad but they are better than the rest
Sometimes I feel sad but don't have a reason
Having a bad day or just bloody freezing
Friendships are hard, I want and try to fit in
But that's not enough and my head starts to spin
I am the first to ask if they are okay
No one ever asks me why I am feeling grey
Every job I've had hasn't worked out
This makes me mad, I want to scream and shout
The world around us right now really is strange
I wish I could but it's something I can't change
My happy places are closed, nowhere to go
The bingo, cinema, even to see a show
Looking through my memories of places I miss
Hoping I get to go back as that would be bliss
Mental health is real, it really is hard
I really need to stay on my guard
This is the story of little old me
Who is struggling along as that is the key

About the Author

My Name is Lisa Murray and I have been writing since January 2019. I joined a writers group and my confidence grew and a new hobby developed.

The Bucketlist Part one is based on a true story, my story.

We see Anna go through many challenges from childhood bullying to college days.
We join Anna as she ticks of a bucket list trip to London and watch her develop an adoration on the city that it becomes not only her "happy" place but her home from home.

Anna gets the chance to live in London not once but twice and finds a new love of Musical Theatre. Book of Mormon and Jersey Boys both becoming a part of her life and she makes connections with both casts.

We also follow Anna as she goes through lockdown when coronavirus hits and she can't get to her escape and happy places.

Anna has depression and anxiety and we see the ways she both deals with this and the struggles she faces to battle these demons.

Chapter 1

"Hurry up!"

Anna grumbled to herself, as she was sitting in Nando's, watching other tables be served. The panic set in. She only had half an hour before the show started. The meal arrived, but no coleslaw – no time to worry. Anna ate her plain chicken wrap, drank half of her juice and headed next door to the theatre. The queue was slowly moving as bags were checked and tickets scanned. She got to her seat just in time as the lights went out and curtains rose. The tears rolled down her cheeks as The Jersey Boys sang, 'Cry for Me' around the piano. The theatre was so silent, you could hear a pin drop.

Interval came. Does she get an ice-cream? She hummed and hawed, then at the last minute scurried down the aisle to get a vanilla tub. She sang and danced her heart out to the finale, cheering every cast member as they took their bow. The show was amazing as always and she loved seeing Michael as Frankie for one last time. Once the orchestra had finished, she made her way out. Pushing her way through the crowd, clutching her Primark bag, she headed to stage door and got her group photo with all four seasons then headed for the bus. But it wouldn't be a theatre trip without disasters after leaving her purse on the bus she had to walk 20 minutes to the bus depot, this is the reason she was late for her dinner before the show and caused the rush but she was happy and enjoyed her day. When she got home, she wasn't even through the front door when she could hear her mum calling from the kitchen,

"Are you wanting tea?"
"No. I had Nando's."
"On your own?"
"Yeah."
"How was the show?"
"Fine."

Anna lived with her parents. This was normal from Anna's mum, asking lots of questions when she got home. While out in town earlier and walking through the shopping centre, she saw a girl who she had gone to school with. They didn't acknowledge one another. She looked 'different,' thought Anna.

School years weren't Anna's greatest years. During school, Anna had thought of Ruth as her best friend. They had sleepovers, went on bike rides, went swimming and even went to the same dance school. One memory always stuck out, though.
Ruth was asked by Mrs. Elliot to hand out the charity box to anyone who had spare change. Reaching Anna and Lola, Ruth joked, "Mrs. Elliot wants your money. She needs a new handbag." Lola laughed, but Anna didn't.
The bell was about to ring when Ruth cornered Anna in the bathroom, saying she had better agree with her, or else.
Anna, out of fear, called Mrs. Elliot a 'thief'. Jo, another girl in the class, overheard and tattled to the teacher. After school, Jo ran straight to Anna's mum who took her to the head teacher to find out what happened. Anna didn't dare tell the truth though so lied and took the blame. Now she was grounded and missed her friend's sleepover. She wasn't happy as Ruth was going, and they were going together.

High school wasn't the best, either. But Anna did enjoy Music and took part in the choir and other clubs including the samba band and orchestra.

On the eve of her 14th birthday, six of her friends came over. They had dinner then sat in Anna's room. When her back was turned, one of the girls broke open her diary and read out aloud. Anna grabbed the book, running down the stairs, shouting at her mum, "I don't want a sleepover, send them all home" Anna leaving her friends in the living room slept in her own bed.

Another event during free period tampered Anna's school years, one day, Anna and her friends were sitting in the breakroom, Anna nipped out, and one of her friends pranked her and hid her bag. Anna burst into tears and told the nearest teacher. Another friendship ended.

One of the hardest events to go through was when her Great Uncle had his legs amputated. Anna wasn't told anything by family so struggled with it all, she took solace in one of her teachers but one of the other teachers in the same department who hated Anna told her to stop bothering Mrs. Andrews about some made up story. Anna was devastated and stopped going to her clubs.

From a young age, Anna loved kids. She was accepted into a childcare course at college. She had only just turned 17 and had just left school. This was a big step. The morning of her first day, Anna was sick. It was nerves. It didn't help she had to rush as she had slept in. Getting into college, after getting lost by taking the wrong turn, Anna spoke to one girl in the reception area and sat with her. When it was time to pick a nursery to go to for placement, Anna picked a local one. That would mean a "long lie", and not much travel needed. However, she didn't have much success at that, either. During lunchtime on her placement, the kids were eating, Anna started clearing up some of the toys as the smells of the food made her feel sick especially garlic. Her keyworker stopped her and ordered her to join the kids at the table. That afternoon, Anna was given the task to do an art activity. Sat at the desk and sorting out the coloured paper and shapes, Anna was asked to help one of the nursery workers, which she did, but left the scissors on the table. A little boy grabbed them, and Anna got into a lot of bother. Anna hadn't completed her coursework for her classes, so this was the final straw. The following week back at college, Anna was asked to leave the course.

Anna loved TV, especially soaps and talent shows. She would never go to bed until she had watched all the shows she had recorded. A new talent show, which Sam and John (her favourite presenters) hosted, was holding auditions in her hometown. She had watched series one so was delighted they were doing another series.

Getting the first train to the venue, Anna was a bag of nerves, it was also her first time being out that far on her own. It was 7.45am by the time she arrived and she was only one there. As the sun started to rise over the river, Anna watched the workers place the barriers outside of the entrance. Around 9am, other people started to arrive, and the queue got busier including people she knew so she was glad of the company. After ticket check at 12, they were still waiting outside. The auditionees had walked in and out of the building all morning up and down the red carpet filming. Finally, around 2:15, it was time to go in. Anna felt her belly flutter. She was so excited. Reaching her seat in the dress circle, she had a great view.

The show was about to start, but Anna needed the loo. She headed out into the corridor, coming across filming. Standing watching, she caught the eye of the presenter. He was gorgeous. He shook her hand and said hello. His accent was stunning. Was this really the same presenter she wouldn't watch on TV as she found him annoying and cringy? As she made her way back to her friends, Alex was all she could think about. Those blue eyes.

As the show began, the judges and presenters were introduced. Anna shouted out, "I love you, John," just as the theatre fell silent. Her friends was mortified and laughed, but Anna was in a world of her own.

A few months later, the show was going on tour with the finalists. Alex was hosting.

Getting to the arena, it was mobbed round the back at stage door. The finalists arrived by coach but walked straight in. Alex arrived by car, didn't acknowledge anyone, but pointed at Anna. "I met you at the auditions. Good to see you again."

Anna felt her legs go like jelly and her heart beating rapidly in her chest. She couldn't afford to go see the show so headed home but felt happy Alex had remembered her.

January came around again, and the auditions were back.

Being the first there, Anna helped one of the auditionees get to where she had to be. Once Alex arrived, Anna walked round to the front. Her friend was running late so she couldn't join the queue. Alex and John were filming near the river. This was the best way to catch a glimpse and Anna somehow managed to get near enough to them to say hello but burst into tears instead when they saw acknowledged her and walked towards her.

Once her friend finally arrived, they were last in the queue. Anna was first there, and now she was last in the building. But it didn't put a damper on her day. Popping to the loo before the show started to film again, she bumped into Alex who was filming in the same corridor they had met last year. The day was saved.

That summer, the tour was happening again with the finalists and Alex hosting. After standing at the stage door all day, Anna received a message from her friend, the same one who was late the day of the auditions, now telling Anna she lied about having tickets and wasn't coming. Feeling gutted and disappointed, she went to leave. Alex arrived just in time and organised a ticket for Anna to see the show. Anna went to the show and felt "special" that she was given the ticket. Anna headed to stage door after the show but got very emotional.

The following day, some girls were going craving in the next town, so Anna went too. When the coach arrived. No one stopped, not even Alex, but he did wave. Anna's aunt had a spare ticket for the show, three rows from the stage, a great view. Anna was crushing hard on Alex. He spotted her from the stage and waved.

Writing poetry was a secret of Anna's, and as she headed home, she came up with some words about Alex.

What can I say? What a guy
That accent, those blue eyes
As bright as the sky
My heart just cries.
So magical in your own way
Thank you for making my day.

Chapter 2

Sitting in the Waverly, the pub where her uncle drank, Anna was celebrating her 21st birthday with her friends who had also turned 21 that week. They had been friends throughout school and saw each other regularly. This was a joint celebration. The drinks were pouring in, and the shots were downed. Anna wasn't a drinker, but she wanted to fit in. A few hours later, coming out of the pub they walked over the bridge to the nightclub but her friend was sick. They walked along and got to the corner and decided not to go to the nightclub, they walked down to get a kebab. Anna wasn't hungry but had chips and donner meat. They sat at the shore for about an hour. Her friend was that sick, they couldn't get a taxi, so decided to walk home. It took them over two hours to get 40 minutes away. When Anna finally got home and collapsed onto her bed. The room was spinning.

Now in August, Anna had been accepted into college to do TV Production. After seeing some TV show recordings, she was very interested and wanted to study something she was passionate about. Not being a morning person, Anna almost missed her train. Reaching college, Anna sat on her own. During the year, the coursework was of no interest to Anna, but she did enjoy the practical work. She really enjoyed working with the equipment and particularly enjoyed editing.

The first half of the year was over, editing was one of Anna's favourite lessons. She would often be the one her classmates came to for help. She excelled in the practical work. Now being back at college after the Christmas holidays her lecturer spoke about a trip to London. Anna was determined to go. That afternoon, Anna was invited to the shopping Centre to interview a TV talent star who was performing at a charity event, this was part of her coursework to work on interviewing. She invited her friend along. They sat in the office on the top floor. Anna was nervous, her hands were shaking, and she couldn't get the cassette to work. She was relieved when it was over but enjoyed the experience.

The day of the London trip, Anna made her way to the station. She was the last of her college class to arrive and had the most bags. On the train, they all sat in the same carriage. Anna sat on her own but had a book with her and listened to her music. Getting to Euston, it was a 20-minute walk to the hotel. Anna was sharing with another girl who she didn't get along with. During the trip, the class had an itinerary they had to follow, but on the last day, they had free time. Anna started her day visiting TV studios in Waterloo, walked along to Leicester Square and Covent Gardens before heading back to the hotel for a nap. She wasn't afraid walking about herself, she actually felt relaxed and content. The last morning leaving London, Anna was heartbroken. She wanted to stay. She felt at home. Isolating herself from the rest of the group, she sat in a different carriage and slept all the way home.

Anna managed to gain a National Certificate in TV Production and was ready for her second year.

As she started her second year, the only positive was using her student card in Peacocks for a twenty-percent discount. She was then offered an opportunity to work with ITV. Her dad dropped her off at the location at five in the morning. She helped the production crew set up on the dock. Anna took a breather to watch the beautiful sunrise. During the day, Anna mainly made the tea and coffee. She did enjoy her day, even though she had to have her dinner outside on her own, as she had to watch the equipment but she learnt a lot watching the crew and how they filmed different angles and what cameras worked better. After this day, she was sure college wasn't for her. The following week, she had an opportunity to work in an editing suite. Anna made the two-hour journey there but the building was very old, and the walls were damp. The toilet was black. The staff weren't the nicest or very helpful either. Anna was put in a room on her own. After two weeks, enough was enough, and she called her lecturer and quit. Now unemployed and stuck in a rut, while out with her mum, she popped into a charity shop and was offered a volunteering role twice a week. Anna loved this job; the other ladies were much older, but she enjoyed their company.

Anna didn't have many friends, but that all changed during a crave, when she met Beth. They hit it off straight away.

After being friends for a few months and as a surprise, Beth booked a coach trip to London as Alex had a new show coming out. They went to Hard Rock Café and had macaroni, but it wasn't worth the money. Now on the coach, Anna felt ill. Her stomach was turning. She was excited but over tired.

Now in London, they walked along the Mall to the TV studios where they met up with two other girls. Brogan was also a supporter and she and Anna had been talking regularly online and she brought her friend along. They had lots in common, it felt like they had been friends for years. When Alex came out around midday, Anna had spent a small fortune on gifts for him, including an expensive watch. Anna loved buying gifts for Alex when she saw him. He was always very thankful. He always told her "to treat herself".

Sadly, the audience for the show was scrapped so the girls headed to Hyde Park for lunch. While walking along a squirrel jumped on Beth's leg. Anna found this hilarious. Before long, and being back at the studios it was eight at night, and the girls had left for their coach. Anna and Beth still had a few hours so waited longer. Finally around half nine, Alex came out, but he was drunk. He still had his suit on from filming, but his tie was scruffy and his shirt half tucked in. He was very chatty. Beth gave them space and walked away. Anna asked Alex about a text she had received saying it was him, she had text this number all night, but he denied it and told her to delete the number. As his car came, he wrapped his arms round Anna mid conversation who was tempted to kiss him but just wrapped her arms round him.

Back on the coach, it was dead. They had two seats each, meaning Anna could sleep. She had been awake for 41 hours.

A week later, Anna was heading to Liverpool this time to see Alex host a new show. Thankfully, the audience wasn't scrapped. She was meeting up with her friend Brogan who she had met in London a week before. Getting off the train, she headed straight for the studios where Brogan was waiting. They spent the day there. Alex came out about 6pm.

The next morning, they were first in the queue. They stood at the entrance from 7am until 12pm in the hope of seeing Alex but sadly didn't. On the spur of the moment, the pair decided to make a Twitter fan account for their favourite host, calling it 'Alex United'. In the studio, they were front row. Alex made eye contact and came over to chat during the breaks. After the show, Brogan went home, and Anna walked to her hotel.

Turning a corner, Anna spotted a group of men, including Alex. She froze, butterflies rising in her stomach. As he turned to walk away, Anna shouted, "Alex!"
But he ignored her.
Anna was gutted. She swiftly hurried back to her own hotel, packed her bag and clock watched the rest of the night. The next morning, Brogan asked her to meet, but she wasn't up to it and sat at the station waiting on her train. She tweeted Alex.
Sorry I made a fool of myself.
He replied nearly instantly.
You didn't. Thanks for coming.
Relief washed over Anna as a smile formed on her face.

London became a regular trip for Anna, mainly for Alex, but she also found a love of musical theatre. Her first show was Billy Elliot, and she had great seats in the stalls. She was content. Trips to London, see Alex and see a show. What could go wrong? Anna had no intention of finding a job. She was on benefits, and this was funding her trips. The coach was cheap which also helped. It was a long coach ride from Carlisle, but it was worth it. She began to write in her notepad

London you have stolen my heart taking my breath away right from the start
You make me happy, you make me content
Every trip is well spent
London, my love in all its delight what a city, what a sight.

Chapter 3

Anna worked at a hotel as a cleaner. With her Mum and the job centre on her back she knew it was time to find a job and on the positive side it would pay for her trips to London. It was a long night at work, the shift was dragging in. Anna snuck down the fire escape and checked her phone, coming across a tweet calling Alex a 'Pedophile'.

Without a thought, Anna replied, "Leave him alone".

The train home after her shift was mobbed. She took her phone out to text her dad and noticed tweets were aimed at her calling her a 'stalker'.

As the weeks went on, Alex was still getting trolled, and Anna was defending him, getting backlash.

Alex was hosting a morning show, and it would be easy to meet him, so Anna made her way to London for the day. She printed out the tweets she had received.

Doing her normal, she walked from the coach station to the studio. Alex arrived just as she did.

Handing over the paper, she spoke softly, "I saw you were getting tweeted, so I defended you, but they started on me. I printed some off." Alex turned to the security guard, laughing.

"What did I tell you about tweeting, Anna?"

He then turned to Anna passing back the paper, saying, "Ignore it."

Anna stood in silence, not sure what to do or say.

After Alex was out of sight, she sat next to a wall. Feeling sick to the stomach, she started crying. The rain and tears made the way down her red cheeks onto her green trousers. The rain got heavier, so she stumbled over to the pub and had a large vodka and coke. Once the rain started to settle, she walked along the road and jumped on a bus to Leicester Square. She rested her head against the window, staring at the sheets of rain.

Before her coach home, she managed to get last minute tickets to go see Jersey Boys. Unable to stomach any food, she sat at the fountain until 6:50. She overheard two ladies talking about the show the rain had eased and was only spitting. Then, Anna made her way to the theatre and managed to get a last minute front row ticket. The theatre was packed. Nipping to the bathroom, she looked in the mirror. Her eyes were puffy, and her cheeks were flushed. However, once the show started, Anna forgot about the real world and was immersed in the show.

After the show, making her way out, Anna couldn't believe what she had just watched. It was the best show she had ever seen. The rain was coming on hard again, so walking along, she jumped on the bus to the coach station. The sleeper bus was about to leave, so Anna asked if there was space, paid the extra fiver and got on. She had the downstairs to herself but fell asleep straight away and slept all night. Back at home, her friends were telling her to delete Twitter as the trolls were getting worse, but she wouldn't.

That Saturday, Anna was helping her gran with her shopping. On the bus home, she checked her phone.

Someone had made a fake account of Alex and was tweeting Anna.

I hate you.

Don't ever come see me again or I will have you arrested.

Go kill yourself, no one would miss you.

Anna was beside herself and went home as quick as she could. She knew the account wasn't real, but every time her phone pinged, she felt sick.

Now home, barely making her way up the stairs, she burst into the bathroom and threw up.

Running a bath, Anna climbed into the soothing water. She noticed herself in the mirror but didn't recognise the person looking back at her. What was happening to her?

Who would miss her? She thought, as she lowered herself into the water. Just as her chin hit the surface, she heard the door.

Anna jumped out, dried herself and ran into her room, burying herself under the covers so no one would bother her. She cried herself to sleep and slept for 24 hours. Only getting up as she heard her dad drilling and went to tell him to "Shut up!"

As January rolled around again Alex would be back in her hometown filming. Anna had tickets and went straight to stage door; she hadn't seen him since November. Sitting at the stage door, she got a fright when a security guard said her name.
"Are you Anna?"
"Yeah, I am."
"Alex had asked me to remove you." Anna stood up and walked away. As she got to the corner, Alex came out and walked the other direction. She felt her legs go under her and tried to lean against the window but missed and hit her head on the side of the door. This made her cry, and she couldn't stop. People were walking past, no one looked in her direction. She was all alone.
Alex didn't do the tour that year so Anna gave it a miss, instead she went to Dublin with her friend Beth for Westlife's last weekend of concerts at Croke Park. They had a great hotel right across from where Westlife were staying, unfortunately didn't get a glimpse but had a great time with other fans. The night of the final concert Anna bumped into Brogan and her friend, they stayed at the back of the standing with them. During "You Raise Me Up" Anna was overcome with emotion and spent the rest of the song sat on the ground. Mel was great with her and sat holding her hand, then helping her up when she was ready to. After the show, Anna and Beth went out a different entrance ending up lost. They bumped into other fans and managed to get back to the hotel. Leaving Beth, Anna headed straight to the airport but was that tired she fell asleep and woke up in a panic, she rushed to the gate to then realise she didn't have her passport with her, finding the nearest guard, Anna was taken back to security where someone had handed it in, this also meant having to go through everything again and just making the gate for "final call".

By the time December came, Anna had joined a celebrity news team on Twitter, writing articles and reviews. She was asked to go the pantomime Alex was starring in. She was booked for London that weekend anyway so said yes.

The train to London was delayed. The hotel was a dive. She headed to Jersey Boys and was out all day, but back at the hotel, she had to phone the manager as the female next door became aggressive. She was moved to the room downstairs. Luckily, she was only there for one night.

The journey to Nottingham was a doddle. The hotel was lovely. A big double bed, and all for her. Getting to the theatre, Anna felt sick. She asked a friend to join her. They had a good view of the stage and were gifted some merchandise – a mug and a programme. After the show, they were invited to the after party. Anna noticed Alex coming in, so she stared at her phone. She could hear him but didn't want to make it obvious. Alex wasn't happy Anna was there and let the organiser know.

"Why is she here?"

The organiser mumbled something in reply, and Alex's entire body language changed. When the organiser walked away, Alex walked straight to Anna, kissing her cheek and hugging her.

"It's good to see you. How you been?"

"Fine, thanks," Anna replied, thinking, you two-faced git!

They chatted for a while, but all Anna could think was her friends had been right about him. They always told her he didn't care as much as Anna thought he did, she was only another fan to him. Leaving the venue, she knew. It was time to move on. She added to her notepad

What have I done? I should have walked away
You used to brighten my day now you turn it grey
I should have listened when I was told you didn't care
I did nothing wrong, this isn't fair
I thought you were different. You were so nice
I travelled far and wide, not even thinking twice

I wasn't special, I gave you my heart you broke it in half, you tore it apart

Finally, some good news came early in the following year. Anna had been offered the job of a lifetime in London. Saying goodbye to her friends and family, she had applied for a transfer with her company, now working in the Hilton in London. She couldn't believe it when her application had been accepted.
She was moving to London.

Chapter 4

Arriving in London at 4:30 in the afternoon, Anna was exhausted. Her adrenaline from the excitement had worn off. Due to train strikes, it would take more time to get to North London. She phoned her new roommate to let her know of her circumstances. "Hi, it's Anna. I should get to the station around 6ish. Can you meet me?"

Her roommate seemed to have other plans. "Can't, it's my birthday and I'm going to meet friends. Get the number 18 bus. It's a five-minute walk from there. I'll leave a key in the pot."

With two cases, a bag on her back, the sweat pouring from her, Anna made her way to the Underground. Reaching the station, the bus was sitting there. Anna rushed and made it just in time. Her leg oozing blood as she had caught it on the case.

Now at her new home, she carried her cases to the second landing. Meg was still there. "Hi, I'm Meg. Did you find it ok?"

"Yeah."

"I'll be back about midnight. Help yourself to anything until you get settled."

Anna made up her bed and took clothes out of her case for tomorrow, falling asleep straight away. She was woken up by chatter and music. Squinting at her phone, she saw it was 2am. She opened her door to see Meg and her friends sitting in the living room. She went back to bed; she couldn't sleep, though, and started her new job in a few hours.

After missing her alarm, Anna rushed to get dressed and out the door, making it to work just in time. The hotel was quite a walk from the station. She waited in the queue to sign in. She said her name, but they had no note of it. She had worked in this industry back at home, so talked her way into being allowed to wait. Now checked in, she took her phone out to text her mum when the supervisor put her hand over it.

"Phones are not allowed, neither is juice." Anna had a water bottle with her filled with orange juice. "Go back and leave them in the break room." Anna was put into position. But she was talked down to, and when customers arrived, the supervisor stood behind her. She felt belittled. During the shift, Anna's throat was dry, making her cough. She went to get a drink of water when she was ordered back to her position. The last hour, she didn't feel great. Her throat was rough, and her chest was tight from coughing. She made her way to the first aid room when she was told she was having an asthma attack. She had asthma for a while but had never had an attack before.

Her supervisor came to see why she had left her position walking into the room as Anna was placed on gas and air to help her breathe. She was then rushed straight to A&E. This wasn't how she saw living in London, alone in a hospital with no one to call.

A week later, Anna was finally starting the job she had moved to London for. She made her way to the station as early as she could and was at the building an hour before she was meant to. She took a photo and added it onto Facebook, #feeling proud.

After her tour, she was asked about the photo on Facebook. She apologised and was told, "Not to worry about it."

She spent the rest of the day transcribing videos. She enjoyed it and chatted away with other staff who made her feel welcome. The job was only for a month, but Anna took a chance and asked to stay on but was told, "Not at the moment but we'll keep you in mind." Was the reply.

Things at home were awful. Meg had friends in every night, and Anna was exhausted. She sat down with Meg.

"I get up early morning for work and feel like it's unfair you have friends in as I'm getting disturbed."

"Leave then," Meg replied. "It's my flat."

Anna left two days later after finding another home. This time, her housemate met her at the station to help with her belongings.

It was Anna's birthday, and she had booked to go see Matilda that night. She had a job interview in South London so made her way there first.
She had dinner at Pizza Hut then made her way to the theatre. Matilda was one of her favourites. She hadn't felt this happy since she moved. She had the London she loved back, dinner and a show. It was March, and Anna had made friends who enjoyed seeing TV shows. She was on her way into central London when sirens sped past her. She met up with her friend who told her the show was cancelled as there had been a terror attack on Westminster Bridge. Anna made her way to Trafalgar Square; it was so quiet and eerie. She sat at the fountain and booked a ticket to go see Wicked. She had never seen it before and needed a distraction. The show was superb, and Anna made her way home. No one was around, and even the Tube was quiet.
April arrived, and Anna was heading to Brighton to see a comedian she enjoyed. She had tickets for both shows so went for the weekend. Brighton was lovely. She walked along the pier and found a church for Sunday mass. Anna decided to head back home to celebrate Easter. She was looking forward to it, but felt a little anxious, more about leaving her grandparents again; she missed them like crazy. Easter Sunday was spent with her family, just like old times.
It was time to head back to London. The train was delayed, and her mum wanted her to stay until the morning, but she had to get home for work. The train took another two hours, but she finally got to London and back home.
It was now May; Anna was sitting in her room sorting her things out for work the next day. Her roommate chapped on her door.
"Turn on the news. Something's happened in Manchester."

Changing the channel, Anna was gob smacked. She sat right next to her TV, not believing what she was watching. There had been a terror attack at Manchester Arena. This was the industry Anna worked in. She had only started working at Wembley Arena as a steward, so everything was too familiar. Every shift started with a briefing, but she would never have believed it would happen and so close. After being awake all night just watching the news, Anna couldn't face going into work, so called off. Would she ever go back?

A few weeks had come and gone, and Anna was finally ready to go back to work to the arena. She felt sick at the thought of it, but knew she had to go back. They weren't allowed phones on position, and Anna was placed on her own. No one came near her all shift, and her pager didn't work. Every little noise made Anna jump. She felt sick and wanted to go home. She had to get out of the building. At the end of the shift, she cornered the manager and told him she felt unsafe. Her manager told her to stop being silly.

The next day Anna had been out shopping and had to rush home as she had a splitting headache. She called off immediately and went to bed. She was awoken by sirens. It was now 9pm. She asked her roommate, "Why all the sirens?" She turned on the news. Another terror attack, this time at London Bridge, only 20 minutes down the road. It all hit Anna, and she burst into tears. If she had gone to work, she would have been at London Bridge, as that's where she changed trains. She felt afraid to live in London, so the next day, jumped on a train and went home for a few days. She really felt silly. She hadn't been caught up in any of it, but it played on her mind, and she was having nightmares. She wrote in her notepad

Woke up on a normal Saturday, climbed out of bed.
Had a quick shower, got myself ready.
Really needed to go to Asda but was working later so had to be back smart As I arrived home, I started to feel sick, put away the shopping, went to lie down. An hour had passed, I had woken up feeling worse.
Messaged my work, told them I wouldn't be in.

Ran myself a bath, made a cuppa, headed back to bed.
It was now nine fifteen, I was awoken sudden, I could hear sirens in the distance getting nearer and nearer. Looked out of the window but everything looked the same.
Turned on my T.V, my eyes were drawn to the bottom of the screen.
Breaking News... An incident on London Bridge
Not another one
Why London why?
I rang my mum and told her I was safe.
As I put down the phone it all became clear
I should have been there
I should be at London Bridge
Sat in my room, sat in the darkness, scrolling through my phone.
The light from my TV lighting up my room.
Lying on my bed, listening to the sirens. As I close my eyes, I thank the lord I felt sick.

***

After a week, Anna was back in London. The attacks still played in her mind, but she wanted to be back in a routine. She was working at an event and some of her colleagues from back home were down for it. She really enjoyed it.

Now on her way to Manchester for another event, Anna was looking forward to seeing and working with her colleagues from back home. She had a great ten days and really excelled in her job. After a long month of work, she joined her friend on a day trip to Blackpool. They walked along the pier before having a fish tea. She took the offer of a lift and headed back up the road.

Now back in London, it was August, and Anna was working on a TV show for the first round of auditions. This was a massive tick from Anna's bucket list. She had watched this talent show from the start and always wanted to work on it. From the moment she arrived at the location, she was victimised. She was pointed at, talked and whispered about. She stayed the full shift but was happy to leave. Making sure she did everything that was asked of her. After a horrible day, she rang her mum, booked a train ticket, quit her job and headed home. She wrote down

I had a dream, it came true
I didn't even have a clue
How hard it would be
But I was jumping with glee
London was my home
Through the streets I would roam It all came apart
It broke my heart
I thought I could do it
Now I must quit
London, you will always be my place where I run to when I need space.

Chapter 5

Now back in Carlisle, Anna was isolated. She had no money, no job, and her friend Beth had moved on. They had been friends for ten years. Beth enjoyed drinking and socialising in pubs and nightclubs. This was of no interest to Anna. She would spend most of the day sleeping and then staying up through the night. She found a love of talk shows in the states, especially Jimmy Fallon and James Corden, whom she had been a fan of for many years. She would live stream both shows at 4:30 and 5:30 each morning. They made her happy.

A few weeks had passed, and Anna's mum had forced her into ringing her old work at the Hilton to get shifts. It was just after eight in the morning, and Anna was on her way to do an early shift. She hadn't slept and had watched Jimmy and James, then had to get ready to leave afterwards. She could see the day far enough. Some of her colleagues weren't best pleased to see her back. They didn't think it was fair she could get back so easily. The morning was spent clearing the rooms on floor 5. She was working with Emily, who had just started. Anna had just cleaned room 502 when her boss Ruth stopped her. Everything had changed in the eight months she had been away, so she had to sort the toilet roll and towels out making sure they were the correct way. She felt she had no one to talk or turn to.

Anna had a new best friend, Jamie; they would go everywhere together and just enjoyed each other's company. Jamie was also a falpal, a Jimmy Fallon fan, so they would live stream the show while on FaceTime to each other.

Anna would tweet James Corden regularly. James had invited her to be his guest at his panel show in London, and Anna begged her mum to help with funds for hotel and coach. This would be her first time in London since she had left. She couldn't wait to get back. It was the day of the journey, and Anna was packed and ready to leave at noon. Her coach wasn't until 9 o'clock that night so she went a walk the spent the afternoon at her gran's. Getting more impatient, she headed into town after dinner. There was a new Marvel film out, so she made her way to the cinema to watch it.

After the film had ended, she departed to the station. The coach was busy, but she had booked two seats so she could sit on her own. She was exhausted and restless, so hardly slept. Finally, in London, she made her way to her hotel. There were strikes on the Northern line, so it took longer than expected. She got to her hotel at 12 and had to be at Elstree at 2, so quickly got changed and made her way there. Now at the studios, the sweat pouring off her as she had run from the station, she made her way to the VIP tent just in time, as they were being escorted to the studio. She got to her seat and noticed "Amy" on the paper. Her surname was correct, though. During the taping, she watched James carefully, not taking her eye off him. She glanced at her phone when she heard him saying, "Where is Amy Kerr?"

There was silence then Anna remembered that was her. She shot her hand up. Making her way towards the front, James held his arms out, and Anna ran to him. They chatted and took selfies. He was everything she wanted him to be. Making her way back to her seat, Anna missed the step and slipped banging her shoulder off the chair. It left quite a bruise.

After the show, Anna was invited backstage. She sat on her own. James came over, took her hand and said, "Thanks for coming." On the way back to the hotel, she messaged James on Twitter, saying, "Thanks so much" and that her name was actually "Anna," but he didn't reply.

The next day, Anna had time in London. She left her luggage in the station, then hopped on the open top bus tour that lasted two hours. She then had food in Leicester Square before heading up to Jersey Boys. It was cast change that night, but Anna had only a ticket for the matinee. Noticing she had been paid, she bought a ticket for the evening show too. She felt sad watching the show. She loved this cast, and they were one of the many reasons she kept going to see the show. The atmosphere in the theatre was unreal. After the evening show, she waited to say "goodbye" to the cast. She left London that night feeling happier than she had been for a long time. Had she made a mistake in leaving the city?

Now back in Carlisle, she was gaining more shifts at the Hilton, but her asthma was getting worse, meaning she had to take regular breaks to gain her breath. This didn't go down well with her supervisors and colleagues who then had to cover for her.

A few weeks later, Anna was on her way back to London. James had invited her to be his guest and watch the filming of his talk show. With the help of more shifts, Anna had more money, and this time she was getting the train. The train was quiet, so she sat at a table and spent the four hours watching films on her iPad.

Getting into London and feeling relaxed, she made her way to the hotel. That night she was going to watch the new cast in Jersey Boys. She was apprehensive about it, as it was her favourite show, and she knew she would miss the old cast. Having dinner in the pub, she talked to other fans of the show. She felt a lot better about seeing the show 40 times when they said this was their 80th. They walked along to the theatre and took their seats; the show was still great, but she did really miss the former cast.

The next morning, she made her way to Westminster for James's show. Even though she had guest list tickets, she still had to queue. Outside the venue, she was recognised by the ticket company. The Alex thing was still a shadow over her in their eyes, and they were rude to her. The seating was different at this taping, so she didn't get to speak to James. After the taping, she messaged James straight away, who invited her to the panel show in a few days' time. This time, James made sure Anna got to see him. It was definitely worth it for Anna, who had used her wages to stay on a few more days

That Christmas, Anna spent the day with her family. Her 30th birthday was coming up, so her mum made little hints her present would be extra special. Sitting in her gran's, she knew her family were up to something as she was trapped in the kitchen then led to the living room. Her mum gave her a box with little quizzes and challenges. At first, Anna guessed London, as she had a shirt and fridge magnet that said London, but that wasn't the surprise. After another few puzzles, it all came clear—she would be spending her 30th in New York. She was shaking, her cousin gave her a shot of vodka to calm her nerves. Feeing teary, she went to the bathroom to compose herself. This was a massive tick off the bucket list. She couldn't wait.

Chapter 6

As her 30th birthday was looming, the planning had begun. Visiting New York was a massive dream come true, so she had a three-page list of what to do when there. Attending a taping of The Tonight Show with Jimmy Fallon was a must and number one on her bucket list.

It was the first Friday in February, and the waiting list would be opening to apply for tickets. Anna was out with her friend, Jamie, but made sure they would be somewhere with a strong signal so she could get on her phone and apply for tickets. She counted down the people before her as it went from 50 to 1 on her phone. She had already written out what she would say for the part where it asked, 'Why you should get tickets?' so when it was her turn, she filled out everything and hit 'submit'. She now had a wait to see if she was successful.

Jamie was a big drinker and often spent her weekends out clubbing. This was of no interest to Anna. Two weeks before her trip, Anna had asked her to go shopping with her, but she ghosted her. She asked again, and the reply said she was busy. Anna went shopping anyway and stopped for lunch at Frankie and Benney's. She came across photos on Jamie's socials to see there was a get together in her flat. Anna messaged Jamie straight away, and got a reply, saying, "I have other friends; I can't just hang with you all the time."

Anna didn't reply.

Going about her day trying to forget, Anna finished her shopping and headed home. She checked Facebook to see a post had been written about her,

I didn't know I had to have permission to have other friends or make plans with other people.

Even though the post hadn't mentioned her, it was obvious. She saw the comments and everyone commenting calling her names. Beth, who she used to be close friends with, was commenting calling her "5 heads". Anna was devastated and blocked Jamie on all socials. She didn't even have the words and got angry with her mum when she asked about her. She wrote down

Another friendship has come and gone. When all is said and gone
Was it them or was it my fault?
Again, my life has come to a halt.
Am I bad company, am I too clingy? Why do they all have too dingy?
All I want is one true friend
It really drives me round the bend.
Is it in my mind, or am I doubting?
Another lonely day, another solo outing. What do I do to keep them by my side? Are there any instructions or even a self-help guide?
Do I need a friend, or can I do it on my own? Being by myself is all that I have known.

**

A week had passed, and it was finally time to go to New York. Not letting anything spoil her trip, she deleted her Facebook app. Anna was ecstatic and couldn't sit still in the taxi on the way to the airport. After security, they made their way to find breakfast. Anna had a roll and sausage at the airport but was sick after eating it. Her mum blamed it on her nerves and excitement. The flight lasted seven hours, Anna had been on planes before, but this was her longest flight. It went quickly as Anna read Harry Potter and watched Mary Poppins, Frozen and part of The Lion King. The hotel was situated right next to Times Square. Having a list of what she wanted to see, Anna went off on her own and walked along to NBC (30 Rock) to have a nosy in the shop and see the marquee, then made her way down to the Disney store. Back at the hotel, her mum was waiting on her. They went to Applebee's for dinner. Anna was starving.

Waking up at 4:30 New York time, it was Anna's 30th birthday. She was sharing with her aunt, so her mum and gran came into the room. She opened cards and welcomed the dollars she received. After a few hours, they made their way to breakfast in the hotel. Not even sitting for a minute when the hotel staff had brought a cake out and sang, "Happy Birthday" to Anna. She was mortified. After breakfast, they walked down to the big Lindt store and Anna spent 30 dollars on a mixture of 100 chocolates. They then went to Central Park and had lunch. That night, they were going to see Jersey Boys on Broadway. This would be Anna's 50th time seeing the show overall, but she was still excited. They chilled in the hotel, then made the way to Taco Bell. Her family weren't that fussed, but Anna really enjoyed her tacos.

They had a great view of the stage at Jersey Boys, but during the show, her gran kept asking questions, and Anna was getting frustrated. Still, the show was amazing.

After the show, back at the hotel Anna made her way through her chocolates.

The next day, they headed out early down to Grand Central station. Outside, though, Anna tripped and landed on her arm. She was in agony. Her mum popped into the pharmacy and managed to strap it up. They sat in the café until Anna had calmed down, then caught the train to the 9/11 monument.

Walking up to it, Anna was overcome with emotion. She remembered watching it all happen in school. The fountains were beautiful, and she watched as some families had arrived to lay flowers. They made their way through the museum; Anna stopped every so often as she was ahead of her family.

Now back at the hotel, Anna was exhausted. Her family was heading back out, but she stayed put.

Anna wasn't successful in the ticket ballot for The Tonight Show, so went for the next option. It was four in the morning; Anna popped into Dunkin' for a tea then made her way to 30 Rock. Times Square was empty. Taking the time to take it all in and took some photos. She was second in the standby line. Once the ticket people came out at nine, Anna had free time. She had to be back for 3pm.

She went on the tour of NBC, seeing the studios for Seth Meyers and Saturday Night Live. She then made her way to Madame Tussaud's, only wanting to see the wax works of Jimmy Fallon. Buying a shirt, she went back to the hotel to get changed and leave her bag as they weren't allowed in the studio.

Now in the Peacock lounge, she took it all in as she was finally getting to see a taping of the show, she would live stream every morning. Anna had a great seat on the aisle, so when a break in the taping happened and Jimmy asked for any questions, Anna shot her hand straight up and told him it was her birthday, and asked could she have a hug? He gave a great hug and smelled great. He was real. Walking down to the desk, Jimmy turned round and told Anna he would get her some "swag".

After the show, Anna was handed a shirt and water bottle as she headed out. She was on cloud 9 and ran to her hotel. Knocking on her mum's door, she was breathless; she took her inhaler and caught her breath. That night she wrote in her notepad

The stinginess in my eyes after no sleep. The eeriness of walking past an empty Times Square.
The excitement of receiving my standby line ticket.
The checking the time on my watch as I pass the few hours I had.
The nerves being back at NBC standing in the line.
The bubbling inside of me like a champagne bottle about to pop.
The tears in my eyes as I was finally in studio 6B.
The tightness of the hug when I finally met Jimmy Fallon.
The pain in my legs as I ran to the hotel. The joy in my heart as a dream come true.

***

Anna was exhausted leaving New York, but just couldn't believe her dream had come true, and she could tick off some of her bucket list. In the airport, she walked around duty free. She came across a keyring that reminded her of Jamie. She hadn't thought about her for weeks, but she missed her. She bought the keyring and unblocked all her socials. She messaged Jamie a long message, apologising. Jamie didn't apologise but accepted the apology. They arranged to meet for lunch the following week. Anna had her friend back.

Chapter 7

Things at work were getting worse rather than better. Anna's asthma intensified, and she couldn't have her own rooms to clean as it would take too long with her having to catch her breath, so she was paired up. Jackie was much older than Anna, she had worked with the company for 30 years and always had her hair in a tight bun, she just didn't care and wasn't sympathetic towards anyone. After a heavy few days, they were working on floor 3 and had two rooms left. Jackie had plans that evening so made sure Anna was on top of her game and sped through each room. Anna felt very breathless but didn't tell her colleague.

Before the last room she asked to go get her inhaler from her bag, but Jackie refused as she wanted to get the last room done. After they were completed, Jackie left Anna to finish the final touches. Anna felt ill and couldn't catch her breath. She had no phone as they had not been allowed on shift, and her pager wasn't working. Sitting on the bed, she started to really panic. Jake, one of the other supervisors, walked past and helped her along to first aid. Anna passed out as she was lay on the bed. Rushed to A&E, Anna was taken straight to the ward and given oxygen. After a rough night sleep, Anna felt much better the next day. Her boss had messaged to see if she would make her shift, and without a thought, she replied with, "I quit."

After a few weeks of recovery, Anna was now jobless. She had no money and no friends, no one checked in on her, and she felt alone. She spent her days in the house, watching Netflix.

Scrolling through Facebook one night, Anna came across a post about a local writers' group starting up. Writing poetry was a big secret hobby, but she had no confidence to ever share her work.

The morning of the first meeting, Anna felt nervous. Her dad dropped her off at the community Centre. Walking in, there were two other older ladies sitting round the table, and after introducing herself, she sat down. During the session, they were asked to pick a colour. Being a big Celtic fan, she picked the green. The homework to write something was to write a poem on the colour, so as soon as she was home, Anna sat and wrote about her uncle taking her to her first game. She had been only four but remembered it like yesterday. Attending every week, a new talent was discovered. Getting positive feedback really helped. Anna made sure she was writing daily.

After a few months, she was invited to the local open mic night. Speaking to an audience wasn't a strong point, as she would often stutter and then panic.

Unable to eat, Anna walked to the hotel, going over her poems in her head. Listening to others, Anna was overwhelmed with the talent. She was next. Making her way to the middle of the room, her top caught on the chair. She sped up whilst reading out her poetry and was glad it was over. During the break, one of the other attendees gave her positive feedback about her poems which left her feeling proud.

Weekly writers' groups and monthly open mic nights were now part of Anna's routine. Writing poetry really helped with her mental health and filled her days.

Still having no job and missing her London trips Anna felt ready to go back to work. Tuesday afternoons were writers' group days, so if she had an interview, this was mentioned as why she couldn't work that day. Unfortunately, for most employers, this was a major setback and caused numerous rejections.

Finally, her luck changed, and she was offered a security job at a TV studio and would be working on TV shows. Plus, she could have her Tuesday afternoon off. Her first month went well, and she was really enjoying it.

One afternoon, Anna had just finished her writers' group when her boss called.

"Can you do a nightshift tonight?"

Feeling worried, as she had never done one, she replied, "I can't, sorry."
Her boss forced her into agreeing by telling her she was still on probation. She had also just returned from a trip to London and hadn't slept.

Making her way to work, feeling tired, Anna arrived at the office. The shift wasn't as bad as she was expecting, sitting behind reception. Anna typed her poems onto a memory stick and watched films, making the night go quicker. She had also just seen Book of Mormon in London and was obsessed with Adam Bailey who she saw as Elder Price and had the soundtrack stuck in her head. The music and videos helped with her creative side. After the shift and getting home, having caught a second wind, Anna made her way to the cinema to watch the new Spiderman film but fell asleep halfway through, missing most of the film.

Things were looking up too in her life. She attended her writers' group once a week and was getting plenty of shifts. Her first wage she spent on a weekend in London. This trip was the first trip she wasn't sad about leaving, as she was finally enjoying her life back at home.

Chapter 8

2020 would be Anna's year. She was still working at the TV studios and getting plenty of shifts.

As her birthday was coming up, she wanted to do something different. Being a massive Disney fan, Anna decided to go on a solo trip to Disneyland Paris. It was midnight, and Anna was sitting ready for her wages to come in. Around 1am, they were finally in her account. She booked a package deal with flights and hotel included. Hitting submit, the payment was rejected. Knowing she had enough, she tried to ring the customer services, but no one answered.

The next morning, straight away, Anna got through and managed to book her holiday. The bank had banned her from taking money out, as it came through as possible fraudulent activity from her account. But it was finally booked, she would be spending her birthday in Disney.

On a high, Anna made her way to work. Not even in the door, and her boss had summoned her to his office. Pulling out a piece of paper, he handed it over. This was an email from John one of the daytime supervisors

Anna is a kind girl; she is friendly to clients and her colleagues. It unfortunately feels like Anna does not want to work here; she takes regular breaks. I know she has health conditions, but I feel these breaks are getting too much.

Anna looking at her boss confused. "He tells me to take these rests or breathers."

Not listening to anything Anna was saying, her boss issued her a warning and placed her on a two-week probation.

With a twelve-hour shift ahead of her, Anna didn't really want to be there anymore, but her request to go home was denied.

The shift was long, and Anna just wasn't in the mood.

The joy from that morning had totally disappeared. She also got home to find out her Aunt was fighting terminal cancer. The best day became the worst.

When the two-week probation was complete, and Anna was back in a meeting with her boss. She just wasn't feeling it and knew her work had gone downhill since their last meeting. She was asked if she wanted to be in this work environment which she replied, "No." Anna was unemployed yet again and had her trip to Disneyland looming. With only her January wages, she isolated herself at home, making sure she didn't have to spend any money.

The morning of her trip, Anna was a little excited. She didn't have as much money with her as she thought she would but was ready to get away. After her mum had dropped her off at the airport, security was empty, so she walked right through. When she had first booked the trip, she had booked the upper deck lounge. This made Anna feel a little better as she wouldn't have to buy anything at the airport.

After being in the lounge for an hour, she walked round to the departures. Heading to the bathroom, she noticed a £5 note next to the door. She picked it up and headed to Boots for a meal deal.

Managing to be first on the plane and get herself setter she was asked to swap with a woman and small child who were sitting in the emergency exit row. She moved but had to sit on the aisle. She liked a window seat and had paid for that seat. She also felt uncomfortable as the plane was full so she couldn't even move or eat her sandwich.

Arriving at Charles de Gaulle Airport, Anna retrieved her luggage and walked to the meeting point. She had booked a taxi and was to go to one of the coffee places where her driver would be waiting, but he wasn't there. Phoning the driver, he had parked at the arrivals, so she had to make her way back. The airport was massive, and the sweat was pouring from her.

Finally, at her hotel and checked in, Anna felt sick. She didn't want to relax though so made her way for the shuttle bus to the park.

She was finally at Disney, Anna headed through security which was a breeze and made her way to Main Street. She didn't know what was running down her cheek, tears or sweat or both, but she was so happy. After taking photos of the castle, she didn't know where to go first.

Looking at the map of the park, she headed to Fantasyland. Walking straight onto Dumbo and a five-minute wait on Peter Pan's Flight, she decided to try It's a Small World. There was a line, but it went fast, and she was on the ride.

It was coming up to six in the evening, and Anna was exhausted. She walked to Big Thunder Mountain, but it was long wait. After her burger and fries at Annette's, she made her way back to the hotel, unpacked and crashed. The next day, Anna was up and showered for eight. She went for breakfast but only had cereal. The shuttle bus was packed, but Anna was on first so managed to get a seat. After security, Anna made her way to the Disney Studios Park and straight to the Frozen show, it was not what she was expecting but enjoyed it. She then made her way to Toy Story land. She rode Slinky Dog.

Not really feeling this park, she made her way out, going to Earl of Sandwich for lunch using her voucher she got when booking the package deal, then went across to the other park. As she got through the gates, the parade was just starting. Finding a spot-on Main Street, she was glad of a seat on the kerb. After the last float had passed, she made her way with the crowd to big Thunder Mountain as she had a fast pass. This was her favourite ride. She spent the afternoon meeting characters, she met Mickey, Pluto and Donald.

Her feet were in agony so before heading out she went on Hyperspace Mountain.

She was glad to get back to the hotel.

Day three was spent in the Disneyland Park, going through the different attractions and getting on as many as she could. After riding Big Thunder Mountain for the third time, she headed back to the hotel.

Day four, and her last day. Today was her birthday. She opened her cards and was happy to see some euros. Heading straight to the park after breakfast. After hearing someone talk about the speedy pass, she headed straight to get one. It cost a bit of money, but it was worth it, as she could use it to get on most of the attractions in both parks. She headed over to the studios to ride Tower of Terror and Crushers Coaster. Over in the main park, she made her way through the attractions, stopping to meet Winnie the Pooh, who was the one-character Anna really wanted to meet. As it was her last night, she wanted to watch the fireworks so had dinner at Plaza Gardens then ended the night standing on Main Street finding the perfect spot. After many years of watching videos and livestreams she was finally seeing the fireworks for real. The projections onto the castle were even better in person. It was magical. The next morning, Anna caught the first shuttle bus to Disney Village to spend the last of her euros. As soon as she got back to the hotel, her taxi driver was waiting on her. She ran up the stairs grabbed everything and got into the taxi. At the airport, there were a lot of people wearing masks. There was a lot on the news about coronavirus.
How bad could it get?

Chapter 9

March 2020, everything was changing. There were no conductors on the trains, and different groups she was part off were starting to cancel their meetings. Anna's aunt had just passed away from her cancer, and now the whole world was going into a lockdown. Her funeral had been restricted to eight people, meaning Anna couldn't attend. They weren't that close, but Anna really wanted to say "Goodbye"

During lockdown, Anna and her mum would go out walking once a day. They would go different ways, always finishing "window visiting" her grandparents. She enjoyed these walks as she didn't get to spend much time with her mum and enjoyed her company.

In April, Anna woke up to an email saying she had been unsuccessful in her college application to study creative writing. She was gutted, as she really enjoyed her writer's groups and felt her writing had improved.

That night, Anna was in her room watching Riverdale when her mum came in.

"Uncle Derek isn't well. Going to the home, won't be long."

This was her Gran's brother he had been in a care home for the last year. Anna visited every week but because of the pandemic hadn't seen her Great Uncle since Christmas day.

Anna shot right up, thoughts going round her head.

Can they go to the home?

Were they asked to go in?

That night, Anna didn't sleep.

The next morning, she headed to the kitchen. She could hear her mum on the phone and could tell she was upset. Once her mum came off the phone, she went into the living room. "Uncle Derek is on end-of-life care."

Anna couldn't even get the words out; she ran towards her mum and hugged her tight. Her mum was allowed into the home, but Anna wasn't. She went back to bed and slept for a few hours.

That night, they were sitting having tea when the phone rang. It was the home to say her uncle had passed away. Anna was adamant she was going with her mum to her grandparents. This was the first time in over a month she was inside her gran's house. She sat in the kitchen so they could keep their distance.

After half an hour, her mum could go into the care home, so Anna went home.

Two weeks later, it was the day of the funeral. Anna could go, even though attendance was limited. The morning of Anna was sick. Her belly and whole body just felt weird. As the service was a closed funeral, she sat with her family outside of the church and watched the livestream. They then followed the coffin to the cemetery. Even seeing the coffin, it still didn't feel real.

After the funeral, they made their way home. She sat in her room and started to write.

It's been two weeks, it feels like yesterday
I remember that night as clear as day
The night we got that call

Those words coming from my mum's mouth
The thoughts that made my mind go wild
The night we got that call
The fear of the unknown, we didn't know you were sick
My heart dropped, we didn't get to hold your hand
The virus took that away

I feel so angry
I am in so much pain
The virus took you away

Today you went to heaven, my nerves are shattered
We couldn't go for a cuppa, we couldn't tell your story
The virus took all that away.

By June, Anna's mum was working from home, so Anna was on her own during the day. She carried on her walks, trying to gain 10000 steps a day. She also found a new love of baking. She really enjoyed making sponges which she would make in the morning then deliver during her walks to family.

The walks were starting to get boring as she was going the same two paths.

Anna was starting to feel isolated; she was turning night into day. She really missed going to the theatre or the bingo.

Once August came around, places were starting to open again. Her driving lessons resumed so Anna made sure she was up in good time. The lesson went well; they worked on the manoeuvres and Anna remembered them. Her theory test was about to run out, meaning she would have to sit it again, but there was a backlog so she would have a long wait. After her lesson, Anna was dropped off at the station. She felt a little anxious about going on a train again. Everyone was wearing masks, but she couldn't wear one because of her breathing, so felt like everyone was looking at her. She was on her way to the bingo. She hadn't been in so long.

Once she got to the bingo, the table she liked to sit at wasn't available, and she couldn't pick her own electronic. Eventually picking her seat, she got back into it. Playing the mini during the breaks and even getting £100 on a full house. She really enjoyed being back and didn't feel anxious once.

It was now November, and Anna had been applying for various jobs. She kept getting rejections until she got a phone call to ask if she was available to cover the "meal shifts" in a call Centre as a receptionist over the next few weeks. It was only three hours a day, but Anna was ready to get back out.

Anna wasn't a morning person so had set alarms for every ten minutes to make sure she was up. Her mum wasn't best pleased, telling her, "Get up!" Getting to the building, she was shown the ropes and sat and watched the screen for the three hours. This would be her job – watching a screen, using a computer, nothing to set her asthma off. She had finally found a perfect job for her. After many failed tries at work in different sectors, Anna knew this time she would be okay.

The next week, there was an announcement of another lockdown. Anna was asked if she still wanted to work, which she was happy to do. She would be out three hours a day, and public transport was quiet. The only negative was the early mornings.

Christmas Day was spent with her family. They hadn't been together for so long, and it was emotional, but she enjoyed her day. Her favourite present was her Apple watch from her mum.

Anna was looking forward to 2021. She had a new job she loved and knew 2021 would be her year.

Chapter 10

2020 was over, and it had been quite a year. Anna started the year losing her job, lost loved ones but was starting a brand-new year in a great place. She was getting plenty of shifts and now getting longer hours.

After work and needing a portable charger for her phone, she walked along to Poundland. The streets were quiet as the lockdown was still going on and only essential shops were open. Just as she got off the train after her shift and walked down to get her dad, she slipped on the ice and landed on her bum. She felt embarrassed and hurried to the car. Now at home, she tried to get her uniform off but couldn't move her arm. Her elbow was sore. Her mum told her to put ice onto it and rest it, but she was in agony. Her dad took her to A&E.

Walking through the hospital, she was given a mask. She felt her breathing getting faster, and her glasses were steaming up. She started to panic just as the nurse came to collect her. She was given a visor instead. She had badly sprained her wrist and was now in a sling for four weeks. Determined, she still went to work as she knew she wouldn't have to do anything and was back doing the "meal shifts".

It was now coming up to Anna's 32nd birthday. As she was working, Anna had no plans, plus the theatres were still closed. She worked her three hours but came home to no electricity, she spent the evening with her grandparents and a chippy tea.

After two years, she had just booked a trip to London. She couldn't wait, but had to put the shifts in. the next two weeks couldn't come sooner.

After a long two weeks working back-to-back shifts, she was finally on her way to the airport. Only going for one night, she only had a backpack with her, so security went quick. She detoured to Boots for a meal deal, then sat and watched the screens for her gate number. When she got on the plane, she started feeling emotional, she read her book to make the hour flight go quick.

Once in London, she rushed through the airport and headed to her hotel. It was in the middle of nowhere.

After sitting in her hotel room for about an hour, she headed for the bus to the station missing it by seconds. Not sure of the time of the next bus, she walked the 40 minutes to the station.

In the heart of London, Anna walked to Leicester Square, which was busier than she thought it would be.

Not sure how to spend the few hours she had spare, she jumped on the open top bus. It took two hours. It was the best decision, sun was shining, and she was home.

After she returned to Leicester Square and changed in the bathroom in Cineworld, Anna had dinner at Pizza Express. As she looked around, she had not felt this content and happy in a long time. After not eating much during the day, she scoffed down her pizza.

It was now the moment she had been waiting for; it was time to go to the theatre. This would her first theatre trip in over a year. As she walked down Shaftsbury Avenue, the theatres in front of her, she was overcome with emotion. Stopping to catch her breath, she was tapped on the shoulder by one of the rikshaw riders asking if she was okay. Laughing she nodded "yes"

Inside the theatre, she just couldn't believe it was real. The lights went down, the curtains and music went up, and Anna sobbed. It was the best night of her life. Getting back to the hotel was a bit of a mission.

The next morning and an early flight, she made her way to the airport. Not judging the time, she made it to the airport but security was busy, so she asked to skip the line and had to run for her flight.

Work was piling in, but Anna didn't mind. The writer's group was back meeting face to face, and she had been working on putting together her first anthology. This was a massive tick on her bucket list. She had spent all week submitting to Amazon.

A few days later, Anna was on her way back to London. This time, she was going for the weekend. As she jumped in her taxi, she got the notification her anthology was live on Amazon. She was about to see Jersey Boys back in the West End after so long. She took a breather outside the theatre and said to herself, "Life is good, I am happy."

Chapter eleven

Finally after so long, things were going great in her work life. She was getting plenty of shifts meaning booking a London trip at least once a month. She had been taken on by the company as a "relief" worker and was getting plenty of work in all three buildings. She got on really well with her manager and colleagues and really was living "The Life of Riley."

Working at least 56 hours a week, Anna loved her wages she would get every fortnight, she could pay her phone bill, pay her mum digs and still have money left over just for her. The shifts would range between Days and Nights. The days would be busy and go in fast but the nights were long. Anna would spend her nightshifts working on her poetry for her writers group that she loved going to and was very lucky to be given a Wednesday off to still attend. The nights would then fly by as she became more productive and her creative side came through.

As much as she enjoyed her work, it was hard going. The work was fine but she was regularly switching between days and nights meaning her sleep pattern took a knock.

It was a Tuesday afternoon and Anna was about to finish her fifth day shift in a row as she was covering and was looking forward to a few days off. Alec, her manager had stopped by and had cornered her as soon as he came in the door. He needed someone to take on Beth's nightshifts as she had Covid meaning Anna would be working the next four nights. Struggling to say "no" as she was that exhausted she made up the excuse that she was taking her Gran to visit her sister and wouldn't get a chance to sleep but was happy to do three nights. Alec called her bluff and gave her a stern talking to explaining what "relief" meant. Anna now scared and with no other option agreed.

The next day she went to her writers group between 1.30 and 3.30 but she really struggled to write anything due to a restless night so just sat and listened. When she got home she was so tired all she wanted to do was cry. She managed an hour's sleep but woke up feeling worse, she emailed Alec and scheduling saying she had had an asthma attack and couldn't go to work and was "sitting" in the doctors waiting to be seen when really she was at home, in her bed forcing herself to go back to sleep, after a good night sleep Anna woke up to an email from Alec. She rang him and told him she was feeling much better and happy to do the next few nightshifts. The shifts were fine and went quick, Anna worked on her next poetry anthology forcing herself to get stuck into it. The last morning though Alec turned up bang on 7 just as Anna was going out the door. He had cornered her again telling her he needed her to cover the gatehouse for five days starting from tomorrow. Anna felt sick at the thought of it but reluctantly agreed. Crying all the way home, Anna's mum told her to get back in touch and tell him she was going away with her family for a few days so couldn't cover.

Alec messaged back with just an "ok".
Finally a few days off.
After two days in the house Anna was bored, Sister Act was playing in Carlisle that week so Anna booked a last minute ticket and decided to have a "solo" night out. She did this regularly and really enjoyed them. She was an introvert but felt confident going to the theatre on her own. Getting off the train, she headed to Wetherspoons. While there she received a phone call from Alec asking to come into the office. She didn't think of work or Alec the rest of the night and enjoyed her escapism at the theatre.
The next morning, Anna felt herself again. She headed into the office for her meeting, he was already there sitting behind the desk glaring at her when she walked into the building. They headed into an empty room on the first floor.

He asked her straight out if "she was enjoying working" which she replied "yes" he then mentioned that he wanted to know the "real" reason for calling off the shifts as he felt like she was obfuscating and wanted to know why? Confused Anna mentioned her asthma and said it was bothering her and she was struggling to sleep at night. She didn't want to say she was "struggling" with the shifts so stuck with her asthma giving her bother.

After a long meeting or what felt like was a long meeting, Anna headed home as she had an appointment at the doctor. She sat in the doctor's room and told him how she felt lonely, that she was using all her money to go to London and was putting work before her health so she could afford to go. The more she spoke it became clear to herself and the doctor "she was suffering from depression" now everything made sense. How can she tell Alec the real reason she was working so much was to fill a hole in her life and that she needed to fill it by going to theatres and London trips on her days off.

Chapter twelve

After her diagnosis of depression, Anna threw herself into work taking any shifts that were offered and spent all her earnings on trips to London.

Jersey Boys, a massive favourite of hers was now back in the west end. Every trip started and ended at The Trafalgar Theatre. The cast were better than ever especially Adam as "Gaudio" and Carl as cover "Tommy".

Unable to stage door because of Covid restrictions, Anna admired from a distance.

Working a seven day and night shift week, Anna was just finishing her dayshifts and would be moving on to nights. She had a London trip booked and couldn't wait for her last night to finish so she could be on that plane. Finishing at 7am and her flight was 9am she hoped Joe was in a good mood and would be in on time he usually came in just after 6.

As she came in for her first nightshift, Alec was sitting at the front desk. When he mentioned the weekend, her whole body went into a panic but Alec asked if she had any plans on her days off? When London was mentioned, that started a conversation.

"You seem to be going to London a lot, why?"

It's my "happy and safe" place. It's where I go to escape.

Alec looking through his emails on his laptop, pulled up a job application for BT tower.

"Have you ever wanted to move there?"

"More than anything, answered Anna. But I tried before and it didn't work."

Alec asking her to sit mentioned how he could get her a transfer to London, 56 hours a week and paid every two weeks. Anna shocked said she would think about it. That she did, all night. She sat and thought about moving to London, checking "spare room" for decent rooms with a good commute to "Theatre land." Getting home, Anna mentioned it to her parents who shot her down straight away, telling her

"It didn't work the last time"
"And she would be back within months". Feeling crushed she cried herself to sleep. Waking up, she knew she wanted to give it another try, knowing this was the perfect opportunity for her so as soon as she got into work messaged her boss and asked to be transferred. Feeling the buzz inside of her.

After her last nightshift, she ran out of work and headed to the airport, reaching London she could feel the ecstasy running through her. It was her favourite trip even though she did what she always did, saw Jersey Boys matinee and Come from Away that evening then another two show day with Les Mis and Jersey boys the following day. She felt like she was walking around in a bubble that no one could burst. Leaving London was always hard, even though she didn't want to leave she felt optimistic and couldn't wait to return. This time to stay.

Back at work, Anna spent most of the shifts looking for accommodation. Finally finding somewhere, she messaged the letting agency and the rest was history, no looking back now. Unfortunately, the process took longer than expected and Anna's anxiety was through the roof. The references took a long time to come back and feeling deflated she booked a little two day break to London after Christmas.

Knowing this, Alec arranged a meeting at BT Tower so Anna could go and see where she was working and who with. This was her first stop, but she stood outside and bought "rush tickets" for Jersey Boys before she headed in. The meeting went well and feeling positive Anna knew she was making the right decision.

It was now the end of January and Anna was finishing her second dayshift. The letting agents had phoned to let her know everything was great and they had everything they needed that the room was hers.

Anna was shell shocked. Without a breath, she rang everyone she knew. She couldn't believe it. In three days she would be moving to London. She had dreamed of this moment for a long long time. Her deposit paid on the room, a one way flight to London paid for. Anna was on cloud nine.

The time came, going round family and saying her "cheerios'" they were emotional especially her grandparents. She knew her family were thinking she was rushing into it but she couldn't pass up the opportunity.

Finally the morning had arrived, after saying bye to her Mum she headed to the airport.

Walking through, she was waiting on something to happen but nothing did.

Walking through Luton with two suitcases and a backpack, getting home for a shower was just what was needed. As she was just in the door rush tickets for Jersey boys went out so that was main priority. Looking around the house, the bathroom was full of mold, the TV didn't work and the commute to London was long and expensive. Anna was a little tired and emotional but as she took her seat in The Trafalgar Theatre she knew she did the right thing. Her dream became a reality

She was living in London.

Chapter thirteen

After a stagey first weekend living in London, Anna was loving every minute. Coming out of seeing back to the future on the Sunday night and feeling a tightness in her chest, she headed home. After tossing and turning throughout the night, Anna got herself ready and walked to the train station. Feeling out of breath as she boarded the train, she dived into her bag for her inhaler. Walking to work, she got lost, she could see the top of the tower but couldn't find the right street to get there. Finally, reaching the staff door, Paul came out as she reached to press the buzzer telling her she would be spending the day in a different site completing a first aid course. Not even catching her breath she followed Paul back to the station. He walked very quickly and it was hard to keep up. Reaching the other site, the other guards were waiting to start. The morning was spent watching the PowerPoint that the lecturer had put together, it was very long. For her lunch break, Anna joined some of the other girls at McDonald's but was more ready for a drink having two large Fanta's.

Back at the site, the afternoon was filled with physical exercises, Anna was paired with Becca, and they put each other into the recovery position and did the Heimlich maneuver on each other. Anna enjoyed this part but felt her chest become more and more tight as the day went on and started coughing more. The last task of the afternoon was working on a mannequin. Anna waited her turn, bent down and took a breath in, but as she did she felt faint and grabbed her chest fighting to breathe. The room was cleared and first aid managed to settle Anna until the ambulance arrived. Now at the hospital, Anna felt very alone, she didn't know or have anyone to ring close by. After a few hours, Anna was discharged and given steroid tablets and inhalers and advised to rest.

After a long day, Anna decided to cheer herself up with a last minute theatre trip, she headed to Trafalgar Square. It was filled to the seams with Men and Women wearing tartan and waving Scotland flags, it felt like it was St Andrew's day in March. Anna sat on the bench with her Tesco meal deal watching the "Football" fans. About 7, Anna walked over to the theatre to escape for a few hours at her favourite show.

After her episode the previous day and a much needed goodnight sleep she took it easy, walked to Lidl then spent the day in bed watching Netflix.

The next day feeling a lot better, Anna was ready to try again and start work. She managed to get there in plenty of time and made a deal with Ruth who told her she would be in early tonight. Anna was paired with Julie who didn't talk to her unless it was giving orders. She did find it easy to talk to Marie and Jack when she went round to the other entrance to give breaks. The day went quick and Ruth stuck to her word appearing just after 6pm. As she was exhausted, Anna fell asleep as soon as she got home. With her shift pattern being three days and three nights, Anna was now on her third day, after work and getting away at 6pm again, she walked to the nearest chippy where she got a free dinner as there was a hair in her food then went to see Come From Away.

The next morning and waking up about 10, Anna walked down to the shop then forced herself back to sleep until 2pm. Nightshifts were very quiet as there were only three guards so Anna spent the night round at the other entrance with Jack who she shared "patrol's" with, doing three each.

Getting home, there was a letter under her door
"Stop using my cutlery and give me back my black mug."
Feeling confused Anna couldn't keep her eyes open any longer. About 9am, there was a bang at her door, shaking as she opened it, her roommate was standing there. He demanded the iron board, Anna had used it and forgot to put it back. Climbing back into bed, her heart was thumping. She placed a chair on the door and managed to sleep until 2pm but just felt shaky.

Chapter fourteen

Going to the theatre on her own just seemed normal, she was used to it. Having her own routine. Living in London meant having Jersey Boys on her doorstep and regular visits, as there were no "stage door" allowed tweeting the cast after the show became routine.

Carl who was first cover Tommy became a favourite, he was scheduled to be on for the full weekend so a Saturday two show day was definitely needed. Finishing Nightshift at 6am and two hours' sleep, 10am rush tickets were bought for both shows. Unfortunately, due to train strikes a longer journey meant not getting to go back to bed as she had to get a coach to London and had to leave within the hour.

Reaching Trafalgar square and seeing "Jersey Boys" in lights above the theatre brought a new lease of life and suddenly she was no longer tired.

The theatre staff started to recognise her often saying "back again" or "you need as season ticket", it was all in a good terms but Anna felt like she was going too much anyway and this made her overthink more, by the end of the day she would have seen the show six times in the two weeks since she had moved to London.

Standing in the toilet queue, Nat who she recognised from "Westlife" days was standing in front of her.

At the interval, forcing herself she went to say "hello" there was a spare seat next to her so she had company in the front row for act 2.

After curtain call, Nat walked towards the door and headed to "stage door", a little shy and standing back observing Adam came out and Anna felt "butterflies" he looked at her and waved. It felt like it was just the two of them in the lane.

Fran and Beth joined them and Anna was invited for dinner, they headed up to Leicester Square and had Italian food, not liking Garlic,

Anna stayed plain and had calamari and chips.

They all had tickets for the evening show and were seated front row.
It felt nice to share the show with someone else, they talked in the interval about how amazing Carl was. After the show they all went to
"Stage door" feeling a little confident Anna said "Hello" to the cast, she was delighted to get a photo with Adam, and Carl recognised her from Twitter and Mark remembered her from the Piccadilly days. Now on the coach home, feeling very at home. One of her favourite theatre days in ages.
After a stagey weekend at Jersey Boys, it was time to go back to Dayshift. A busy weekend meant hardly any sleep as her body was still on nightshift mode and Anna was now feeling the strain.
Getting to work at her usual 5.25am, Wilma was already away and Sanji left when she got there. It was now 6.45 and Julie still wasn't there, phoning scheduling Anna wanted to make sure it wasn't one of the agency staff working as they were usually on time.
At 7.20, Julie finally came walking in and immediately started giving out orders. Feeling more and more tired, Anna told her colleague to maybe go and do a patrol for once. Julie getting wound up, started to go on about not being happy that Anna was leaving work before 7. Anna left when cover came in as did other staff but didn't give the chance for Julie to leave as she was always late.
After three dayshifts and getting more and more annoying, Anna was now off as she was heading home for "mother's day" she had always tried to get this day back in Carlisle as her brother lived in the states and she didn't want her Mum to be on her own. Reaching Carlisle and missing London, Anna counted the days until she could get home.
Now back in London and a long three dayshifts, Anna called off her nightshifts, Julie was really getting on her last nerve and it was hard to work with. Now having six days off, going through her list of shows to see and having a much needed rest, it was the London she fell in love with.
A few weeks later and her three days off being the weekend of

Easter. Anna booked a weekend home to see the family, she didn't feel at home in Carlisle anymore but did miss her loved ones especially her grandparents who she would see every day.
Heading back to London and as her flight was delayed it was later than expected to arrive home. Dayshift the next day wasn't fun and didn't help that Anna went over on her ankle out on her patrol. Two weeks later, her ankle was sore as ever, Anna spent her afternoon at A&E. she had broken her ankle and had to wear a boot. Heading straight to nightshift, Julie was late again and once again gave orders.
Walking out on her patrol, she said something and Anna said under her breath "I know where I would like to put the boot."

Chapter fifteen

Getting round London was hard enough at times but now with a broken ankle and having to wear a massive boot it was ten times harder.

It was now two weeks since Anna had been told she had broken her ankle, she was still going to work but had limited tasks she could do which made Julie even more irritable as Anna couldn't do external patrols especially during nightshift. This meant Julie actually had to go and do patrols instead of sitting in the office giving out orders.

The next week, Julie was away on holiday and Anna was left in "charge" she gave out regular breaks and shared tasks between everyone doing as much as she could herself. It was such a better environment and enjoyable shift.

A broken ankle didn't push the theatre trips to one side either, still doing three day shifts and three nightshifts after the last day shift Anna would often go to the theatre after work mainly to keep her awake but also a great way to split up the week. After a great three days without Julie, Anna headed to Trafalgar square, not feeling that hungry and with a Tesco meal deal she sat in the square "people watching" for nearly an hour.

Heading into the Trafalgar Theatre, there were the usual "welcome back" "you know where you are going" and "what number show are you on now?" walking down the stairs Beth who she had met a few weeks ago was standing near the cast list, Anna waved over but Beth turned around ignoring her.

That night, Carl was on for Tommy and Ben was on for Gaudio so luckily "rush tickets" went the right way for her and she was front row. At the interval, Nat was standing at the bar but walked away when she spotted Anna coming her way. It wasn't until she was on her way home that the idea of "going to see Jersey Boys too much" came back into her mind.

After three nightshifts, Anna now had three days off, and it was the weekend, not sure what to see and looking on TodayTix, Book of

Mormon kept coming into her mind. As her foot was hurting and not much sleep after work only the matinee was booked. She had seen the show only once but a few years ago, it had been on her list for ages. Getting to the Prince of Wales theatre, the front of house team were very welcoming, sitting in the circle was a bit of a squeeze but the show was great and she hadn't laughed that much in a really long time. During the interval, checking today tix there was a single front row seat in the stalls for £45, so without any thought it was booked. After the show, Anna headed up to poppies chippy then headed back into the theatre, even the front of house saying to her "Back again" didn't phase her. Front row was such a different experience, so many interactions from the cast. After the show, standing at stage door with her programme to be signed most of the cast stopped and "welcomed" Anna to the show. Her heart felt very full, she hadn't been this happy in a long time.
The next day was a Saturday and without a single thought booked a double Mormon day. Again she felt really happy and managed to get her
programme fully signed. The next day was a Sunday and feeling exhausted Anna had no other choice but to rest and stay in.
The next three days were back to work, but Julie was back and Anna was back not enjoying her job anymore. It was hard to work in that environment. She complained to both managers but nothing was done and it all came back on Julie's complaints saying that Anna's workload was limited and she was still leaving before seven.
Using her foot as an excuse Anna called off her last dayshift and all three nightshifts. Wednesday would have been Anna's last day but as she didn't go in she booked a matinee of come from away and evening at Book of Mormon.

Weirdly Jersey Boys didn't come into her mind when booking shows, she still liked the casts' tweets and Instagram posts but the thought of actually going to see the show never crossed her mind, she had found a new "happy place" and didn't have to feel uneasy anymore.

Chapter sixteen

Living in London was everything Anna had always dreamed of, it was always a place she could escape, and she didn't have to worry about messaging anyone to go and do something, she actually preferred being away from everyone and could live her own life. There was lots to do and no time to feel lonely. Working in the tower she enjoyed the money she would get every fortnight but due to her work relationship with Julie and taken more "sick" days, the money was going down. Working three days, three nights and adding in going to the theatre meant no rest days. No fault of her own but living in

London Anna was still in that bubble of wanting to enjoy her days off and fill it with what the city had to offer. The managers at work were okay and easy to get on with but wouldn't listen to any complaints she had about her supervisor and how hard it was to work with her.

After being away from Jersey Boys for a few weeks, the news of a cast change happening and most of the cast leaving meant Anna started to go back, she got on really well with the cast and often spent time after the show having a chat. Anna had actually bought her ticket for cast change night back in early May when she was told.

Counting and working out her schedule for work the night would be on her second night shift. When she booked the ticket, she added a holiday straight away, she was happy to go in the next night as expected a late night and would sleep all day. It still wasn't accepted but Anna knew this and wasn't panicking as it usually wasn't accepted until nearer the time.

As the end of June was approaching, Anna messaged the schedulers to ask why her day off wasn't accepted and was told "the holiday will not be accepted, Jack had already taken that day off and there can't be two officers off at the same time" This made Anna feel deflated, it was never a problem before but because of the break-ins the rules were now changed. The ticket was booked at least a month ago. It was expensive, the cast meant a lot to her and she was also at the end of her tether with work. As much as she tried to make Alec understand, he just wasn't budging. After a horrendous week at work, Anna made the decision to message and tell him she was done. She would work another two weeks but that was it. Not even thinking about it, Anna got on with her work and kept herself to herself. As the last two weeks went on, the right decision was definitely made and the countdown was on for her last shift.

To make herself feel better, Anna went to both Jersey Boys and Book of Mormon more often, if there were no rush tickets, normal tickets would have been bought costing Anna at least £80 a show, money she should have been keeping for rent. Jersey Boys visits were much better too as she had made really good friends with Mother and Daughter Kirsty and Sarah. They weren't always at the same show but when they were they made sure Anna got her photos with the cast. She also met Andrea who came to the shows too. It was nice sharing the show with other people who loved it as much as she did.

The time had come, it was Anna's last week working at the tower, and an old friend has invited her to The Late Late show with James Corden that was filming in London. Anna adored James, he had invited her to both a league of their own and The Late Late London show in the past and had met him four times. Unfortunately, the day of the filming was after a nightshift and no time to go home meant having to stick around central London until Carol arrived. Anna didn't apply for tickets herself as she knew she wouldn't get them, but even though she was going on someone else's ticket, she felt sick at the thought of going, one of the management still held the "Alex" thing over her from a good few years ago and she knew in her heart if he was there he would make her day a living hell. Getting into the queue, the anxiety kept building and building even when they were given their wristbands and on the way inside, the thought of something going wrong was getting too much. Getting into her seat in the studio and seeing the show name in lights Anna was overcome with emotion, as soon as James came out the sobbing got more and more and she couldn't stop. On the last link of the show, Anna turned round to see James walking towards where she was sitting, she watched him closely and caught his eye, and he grabbed her hand and said "so good to see you Anna, so happy you got in." now she was in total shock, it was the best day of her life. After the show and meeting James again at stage door, Anna made her way home, she had been awake since 2pm the previous day but she was floating on cloud 9.

The next morning, waking up Anna knew she had two more nightshifts, still being on a high Anna rang scheduling and called off both nights. She no longer worked at the tower. Instead of work, she spent both nights at her favourite shows, it wasn't until Karl had asked "what's next?" Anna started to think
I live in London, no job and no idea what was next!!

Chapter Seventeen

Now unemployed in London, there was no other choice but to job hunt preferably working Monday to Friday but after talking to some of the front of house team at Book of Mormon Anna imagined this would be something she would really enjoy. After many applications to London theatres an interview came through for the Sondeim theatre where Les Mis was currently playing. Due to train strikes, Anna had to get a coach into London, her boot had finally come off her broken ankle so this meant being in a lot of pain. She hobbled along. Making her way to the theatre, the idea of working and doing what she loved made her anxiety through the roof, she really wanted the job. Reaching the theatre, the reception area was filled with young people, Anna was in her early 30s but it was mostly early 20s who were there. During the interview, Anna felt very incongruous, 80% of the interviewees were musical theatre students, and Anna loved musicals but preferred watching them. She felt very out of place.

Using her times as an audience member, talking how she would deal with etiquette and making going to the theatre as magical and an escapism as she felt when she went worked her way through the afternoon.

Wishing she could have went to an evening show and if it wasn't for train strikes probably would have but the next day was West End Live in Trafalgar Square and more train strikes meant an early rise so an early coach home was the only option. She knew a long day was looming and needed all the rest she could.

The next morning, Anna made her way to the bus station, it was just coming up to 6am. West end Live was always a dream to attend but as she was never around London at the right time meant even train strikes couldn't keep her away. Reaching Trafalgar Square Anna joined the accessible queue, with her foot and also having anxiety being in the quieter zone meant she could enjoy the day. Sitting in a seat on the front row but when it was busy, the stewards kept coming up to Anna asking what her disability was. Eventually being left alone,

Anna loved the day. All or her favourite shows on one afternoon. After the event had ended, Anna sat at the wall at stage door and said hello to the Jersey Boys cast, not wanting to go home she booked a last minute ticket to see Only Fools and Horses, it had been on her list for a while but not one she was in a rush to see. £13 ticket did help though.

The show was good but she had never seen as bad etiquette in her life, so many people going to toilet, people talking and looking at their phones during the show then a show stop finished it all as audience members were shouting out and the actor who played "Del Boy" stopped the scene until they were removed. It was ticked off her list but she wouldn't rush back.

After the show, the bus to Victoria was mobbed. Forgetting there was a concert in Hyde Park, two of the coaches were full when they passed where Anna was waiting, and it was now 3am when finally Anna was on her way home, she had every intention of doing day 2 but by the time she got home it would have been time to head back to London and there was just no way that was happening or she would last all day with no sleep.

Trying to keep her money, Anna spent her days at home, in her room feeling really isolated as she didn't talk to any of her housemates and getting rejections daily she fell deep into a depression state and slept the days away. The next weekend was

Jersey Boys cast change, Anna was dreading it, the cast meant so much to her, Mark who had been in the show since the Prince Edward days was leaving and the idea of him not being in the show made Anna feel really sad. Unable to see any more shows during the week due to her funds meant she missed some of the casts last scheduled shows as their covers. The day of the show, Anna had booked a Harry potter walking tour around London, it was free and being a massive Harry Potter fan meant this was the best way to keep her mind off it. The tour was great and the speaker of the tour was impressed with Anna's knowledge of both London and Harry Potter. The tour finished at 5.30 and her ankle was killing her so she sat at Jersey Boys stage door wall until the doors opened. Carl who she had grown very fond of stopped to say "hello" all the emotions came out, Elliot arrived and they both waited with Anna as long as they could. She was very thankful.

When the doors opened, everyone Anna had spoken to both at the shows and stage door were there. She was happy to be sitting with Debbie and had Nat, Beth and Fran in front of her and Kirsty, Sarah and Andrea along the row. The show was amazing, it was nice to see the full cast again. It was very hard though to watch Adam who was a massive favourite of hers as he was very emotional especially during act 2. After the show and during curtain call, Ben gave a speech. As soon as Mark was mentioned Anna lost it, it was in that moment it all became real he was really leaving. Meeting all the cast at the stage door, Anna took her moment to "Thank" Adam for making her smile over the months. He wasn't leaving the show thankfully but it was the perfect time to say it.

The following week, Anna spent all her money at Jersey Boys as her 100th show was vastly approaching. The day of, she had an interview at the Novello theatre where Mamma Mia was playing Kirsty, Sarah and Andrea came to meet her, they went to Poppies for food then made their way to the theatre. Anna had seen the new cast before and absolutely loved them especially Luke who

took over Frankie and Joey who she remembered from the Piccadilly days but this was the first time her friends had seen the new cast, they were big Ben fans and spoke how they were nervous watching without him. They all sat in the front row, as soon as Luke came on Sarah and Kirsty teared up, after the show at stage door they mentioned how the new cast were nothing to the old cast, just as Luke came out and walked over to say "hello"
Kirsty mentioned Ben and how they were the makers of his fan page, feeling a little uncomfortable Anna quickly changed the subject and mentioned Luke almost falling over during "Beggin". Anna's night was made when Karl came over to congratulate her on 100 shows and gave her the biggest hug.
The next morning, still feeling really great, Anna woke up to a phone call inviting her to work on a construction site as a receptionist. She was delighted especially when they were ok that she was heading home to see family and would keep the job open for her. She celebrated with a trip to Jersey Boys.
At last, things were turning around. Anna 1 - Mental health 0.

Chapter eighteen

Working full time again, Anna was getting herself back on track. She would work Monday to Friday days and was getting a weekly wage. After falling behind on her rent she was paying weekly as much as she could, unfortunately, the site she was based in was on the other side of London and this meant paying £150 a week for a travel card. She enjoyed working as the mornings were busy and the afternoons she could just chill until someone needed her.

Westlife were finally playing Wembley on the Saturday after waiting three years, Anna couldn't wait, she was going on her own but she knew Laura and her friends were going too, the Friday before Anna was finishing her shift when Max her boss stopped her, he asked "if she knew the job was only temporary for six weeks" Anna had no idea, when Max left she sat back down staring through the window thinking "what now?". That night she went to see Book of Mormon, Phil was on as Cunningham which didn't happen often as he was second cover. He was brilliant. After the show, Stevie came right over to Anna and asked how she was, she mentioned about her job being only temporarily he told her "something will come up" and hugged her that tight Anna felt like he was squeezing all the air out. The next morning, Anna put her worries to one side, it was Westlife day, as Laura and her friends were still travelling down, Anna booked a rush ticket for Jersey Boys, unfortunately it was up in the circle but the front of house manager managed to find a seat in the stalls for her to move down to. After the show, Elliot mentioned that Mark was coming back for the evening show, if it wasn't for Westlife she would have stayed.

Getting to Wembley, Laura and her friends were waiting on Anna, it felt like old times. The show was amazing and seeing her favourite band in front of her after so long. It was the best way to spend a Saturday, the only time she felt sad was when Laura and her friends stood with their arms round each other but Laura changed position with Emma and wrapped her arm round Anna including her.

After the show, it was a nightmare to get home, feeling exhausted

Anna was glad to get home. She was bursting for a pee and headed straight to the bathroom but the door was locked. Chapping the door there was no answer and her roommate came up out of his room told Anna he had locked the door as someone was leaving a mess in the shower. Anna now in agony grabbed the keys from his hand and went to the loo. She came out and told her roommate to "get over himself."

The next day Anna's body was giving up on after a long day at Wembley. She headed into London Victoria and walked round to Buckingham Palace, she was early for her tour time so sat "people watching." Feeling the strain in her legs she hobbled into the tour. It wasn't a guided tour so Anna took her time walking round, sitting on the benches listening to the audio she was given. After the tour she sat in the gardens and had a scone and can of raspberry lemonade. Looking over the garden she felt emotional and closed her eyes praying for a miracle.

The following week at work she knew the weeks were flying by, Anna had previously booked some shows all the one week. On the Friday, she had Book of Mormon,

Saturday she was at Book of Mormon in the afternoon and Jersey Boys at night, Sunday was her first time at the London Palladium to see Mark Feehily in The Secret Garden, and getting there early Anna sat in the café until Fran messaged to say she was walking towards the theatre. The show took Anna back to her childhood, it was one of her favourite stories and films. The next two days, one of Anna's favourite Broadway singers had concerts in the theatre royal. The Monday show she was going on her own so after work headed to Covent Garden. Sitting at the back of the stalls, Anna moved to second row after the interval, even being that close to Jeremy Jordan, she couldn't believe he was real, listening to Jeremy or watching YouTube videos was part of Anna's daily routine.

Being at work on the Tuesday, Anna was struggling. She had been at the theatre since Friday and it was now Tuesday, tonight was the second and last night and she was going with Fran. Waiting on her friend, Anna noticed two men walking towards her it was Jeremy

...dan and Benjamin Rauhala. Unable to talk as she was stunned, Anna got her photo and in a flash he was gone.

Getting home late because of trains, Anna was exhausted. She almost throwing her phone when the alarm went off at 4am the next morning.

A few weeks later, Book of Mormon cast change was happening. Anna was dreading it, she had growing really fond of the cast. The day of the show was a Saturday so she did two shows, Anna sat in the front row and got talking to Vinnie who was also a big fan.

Vinnie helped her get her photos with the cast both after the matinee and after the evening show. After the cast had left, Vinnie, Tina and Anna stood talking for almost an hour not realising the time until the stage door worker came out to leave. It was great to talk to fans of the show who understood the adoration Anna had developed for the show and cast.

A few weeks later, it was getting closer to being Anna's last week at the site. Still job hunting, Anna was getting daily rejections and just felt lost.

After a busy morning, her colleagues were having a "burns day" for a colleague who was moving to Glasgow with Scottish food and music.

Anna put on her phone to a notification about the Queen being poorly and that the Royal Family were rushing to be by her side. Anna and her colleagues stopped the celebration and sat watching their screens the remainder of the shift. Anna had just gotten home when BBC news announced the death of the queen. Anna sat on the edge of her bed watching the TV. She rang her Gran for a chat, she had only spoken to her a few days ago but it felt like the right thing to do.

The next day after work, Anna headed straight to Buckingham Palace, it was stowed and she could hardly get past anyone, no one spoke, it was really quiet, people laying flowers, taking selfies or paying their respects. Afterwards and before she headed to the theatre she sat in the pub, when King Charles made his speech no one spoke, everyone stared at the TV screens.

A few days later, the queen was lying in state in Westminster Abbey,
Anna was lucky to get into the accessible queue where she waited about two hours she managed to get into the queue for the Abbey straight away when she walked down. Meeting Joan in the queue, they talked to other people but as soon as they got into the abbey no one spoke. It was a moment in history. Walking through with the coffin in the middle, there were two lines sweeping past all taking turns to pay their own respects. Joan got emotional, Anna grabbed her hand, no words were spoken but she could see it meant a lot. Passing a photo of the queen, Anna stopped and whispered "Thank You" before continuing home.

Chapter nineteen

Now unemployed again, Anna was stuck in a rut. She wasn't getting along with her housemates. She felt very uneasy when she saw them and was getting blamed for things that wasn't to do with her. Using the kitchen, Geoff became elemental thinking that because he lived there the longest he had the right to tell Anna when she could use the oven. Anna stuck to microwave meals as they were quick to make and she didn't have to spend much time in the kitchen. Having no money meant being home more too. After booking a ticket to Magic at the musicals at the Royal Albert Hall, Anna had enough money for the train there. Once she got off the train across the road was the Mormon Church, getting caught taking a photo, Anna went for a tour around the church. It was all quite overwhelming as everyone was overly nice, her mum phoned just in time and Anna took the chance to leave. When she joined the queue at the Royal Albert Hall she couldn't get her ticket up on her phone due to the signal and unable to connect to the Wi-Fi. Being sent to different doors Anna was finally sent to the box office who gave her an actual ticket. They did mention not to use See Tickets again as they would let her in this time but she might not be as lucky the next visit. Sitting in the box at the side of the stage, Anna ended up front row. Jersey Boys were performing and when Luke came out to sing "Can't take my eyes off you" Anna felt very emotional and proud, Luke had no musical theatre training and had just joined Jersey Boys making his West End debut after touring with the show as alternate Frankie.

After the show, Anna stood at the stage door, Ben came out first and walked straight towards her giving her the biggest hug. Adam and Luke came out together and Adam wrapped his arms round her. After Karl came out, Anna made her way home.

The next day was the queen's funeral so Anna spent the day at the nearest cinema watching it all. It was still very surreal. There were no stalls open for snacks and the cinema was eerily quiet. After a long week doing nothing but job hunting, Anna booked herself a ticket to see "don't worry darling" at the cinema. After finishing her drink early Anna walked out to the front to get another drink but as she came back her bag was missing. She hunted everywhere when the guy behind her mentioned one of the staff had lifted it, when she got it back it was a Polly bag but it was soaked and her belongings were covered in coke. The guy mentioned they had no time to clean the screen after the last one so went to do it as the film was starting. He put a half cup of juice into the bag. Not even one bit apologetic, Anna took out her jumper that was soaked, put it back in the bag, binned it and asked for her money back. As her brother was visiting home after being away for a few years, Anna headed home. She felt very secluded as everyone was more interested in Zack than her. As she headed back to London she wondered if there was any point, she was jobless, no money and about to lose her room as she was behind on her rent. While at home she also learned her Uncle's dog had been put to sleep, no one had told her and she felt sad she didn't know so was glad in a way to get back to London. She lasted another week, on her last day she headed to London to see Book of Mormon matinee, after the show she mentioned to the cast she was heading home for a while, they were all lovely, wished her well and gave plenty of hugs. That night she headed to Jersey Boys, sitting front row she wanted to sit with her friends but the couple next to her wouldn't move up one seat. Feeling very emotional during the show which some of the cast saw so Luke made it extra special for her pointing during "working my way back". At stage door, every cast member made a beeline for her, wishing her well, giving hugs and asking her to "hurry back." Her heart felt very full. The next morning Anna struggled to the station, she was offered help with her bags but when she got to the station, the man hit on her and made her feel uncomfortable. Sitting at the station, she just felt sad, disappointed and lost. As she looked out the train window when they pulled out of Euston station she wondered if maybe her story wouldn't have a happy ending.

Chapter twenty

After being back in Carlisle almost a week and a half, everything was going wrong and Anna had never felt sadness like it. When she visited family, she was mocked and laughed at when she mentioned going back to London. Told "to give it up" that she had "tried and it didn't work yet again" even going out and about Anna was asked "if she was up for a holiday?" "How long she was up for?" this made Anna stay in her room with the door closed turning night into day and vice versa. It was a Saturday night and Anna was in alone as her mum was out. She had a full list of programs to watch so went for an early bath. She could then just chill the rest of the night. Not realising the time and being in the bath for a while as she was reading her book, Anna jumped out and got herself changed. Realising she had left her phone in the bathroom, she ran into get it but as she got through the bathroom door, her foot slipped on a wet patch and with a thump she fell to the floor, luckily she didn't bang her head but gave herself a fright and in a deep shock. Trying to get herself up, Anna tried to grab onto the radiator but it was roasting, finally she managed to shuffle to the nearest bedroom and shuffled her way to the bed, she picked up her phone and called her gran. With her mum being out she didn't want to disturb her. Her gran told her to get her dad who took her straight to A&E. She was taken round to minor injuries where she sat for 30 minutes before being seen, given painkillers, did a urine test then waited another 30 minutes in the ward. Eventually, she was told to head round to the main area where she sat for two hours, having to stand up regularly as she couldn't sit long. The doctor gave her medication and told her "it was muscular" she would be in pain for a while and sent her on her way. Anna not sure what to do as her back was that sore got on with it but cried herself to sleep nightly because of the pain. She needed help getting ready especially the bottom half with her trousers being the hardest, she also had to wear shoes she could slip on and off.

A few weeks later, Anna went back to the writers group, for the first time in weeks she was happy to be "home" and felt like she belonged again. Her creative side came flooding back and she started writing more, working on poems for the group and also started writing a book about her, she had so many stories to tell so turned them into fiction, she also read a chapter each week at the group getting feedback and giving her a new lease of life as she had something to work towards.

Also being unemployed and back on universal credit, Anna started job hunting, her back still being in mortal agony meant Anna having to limit what jobs she applied for. One of the jobs she had applied for in London before she left had emailed her, asking her to come for an interview, being skint Anna asked her mum for help with money but she said "no"
At her job centre appointment it was mentioned. They agreed to pay for the travel. Anna rushed home and begged her mum to pay for accommodation which she did. She was going back to London, only for 24 hours but she was going back to London.

It felt like Christmas Eve, her train was at 8am but Anna couldn't sleep. She was up and ready the crack of dawn waiting to leave. On the train there, Anna read the whole way meaning the journey went quick, reaching Euston station Anna felt elated, not even her back pain could spoil this.
She was home.

After her interview, her friend Gemma messaged to say she had bought two tickets to book of Mormon and hoped Anna was free. Anna felt like she could burst. Sitting in Leicester square it felt like old times, watching the street performers and tourists.

Once Gemma arrived it was just like a normal theatre night, they went for food before walking down China town to capture the best view of the Prince of Wales theatre. Some of the Front of house team remembered Anna and welcomed her back. After the show, Ben and Tom were doing a meet and greet in the foyer. This was the last time Anna would see Tom as Cunningham and it all became real as he hugged her so tight. The rest of the cast all welcomed Anna back, it was like no time had passed. That night, the accommodation Anna had was fine but the bed was so hard it was like sleeping on bricks. This meant no sleep, the next day Anna managed to get second row for Jersey Boys for £25. This show was her "safe place" she was manifesting being very emotional and hoped the cast missed her as much as she missed them. That they did, after the show she met most of them, Luke also popped out to see her before he warmed up.

As soon as Adam left to go for food, it all became clear to Anna she had to leave. She didn't want to, it was everything she needed to be back in London with her friends and having her "happy show" and "safe show" where she needed it.

Reluctantly she got on the train and managed to get a window seat. She was sad to go, she knew deep in her heart she would be back. As the train pulled away she got an email from Amazon to say "The Bucket List" was now live on Amazon. Her story was out there, she did have a good life but she was the way she was because of different things that had happened to her. She remembered three lines from Book of Mormon

The past is all in Tatters
But today is all that matters
Tomorrow is a latter day

Printed in Great Britain
by Amazon